Lee was staying at Kipper's house for the night.
"I wonder if the magic key will glow while you're here," said Kipper.
"Me too!" said Lee, who had never been on an adventure.

The boys went to Biff's room to check on the key.

"I'll let you know if it starts glowing," Biff told them.

"Do you want to play a board game until then?" Kipper asked her.

"No, thanks," said Biff. "I'm at an exciting bit of my book. The heroes are running away from some hungry ogres."

Lee looked at the book's cover. "What are ogres?" he asked.

"Horrible monsters!" said Biff.

The boys went to Kipper's room. After he put his sleeping bag on the floor, Lee peeked in the wardrobe.

"What are you doing?" asked Kipper.

"Just checking," admitted Lee. "For monsters."

There was the sound of footsteps coming down the hall.

"What's that?" asked Lee. He was a bit jumpy now he had started thinking about monsters.

The door opened.

It was Biff.

"Come quickly," she said. "The key just started glowing!"

Kipper jumped up. Lee followed more slowly, feeling a bit nervous. What if the key took them somewhere scary?

Lee watched Biff pick up the glowing key.
"What happens now?" he asked.

Before Biff or Kipper could answer, the magic
began to take them away on an adventure.

The magic took them to a deep, dark forest.
A bitter wind howled and made them shiver.

"What now?" Lee asked.

Biff shrugged. "We'll soon find out why the
key brought us here."

Suddenly there was a booming noise.

"It's an earthquake!" cried Kipper.

"No," said Biff. "Those are footsteps, and
they're getting closer!"

Lee's eyes opened wide. If those were footsteps,
some big feet were making them.

A huge head appeared above them.

"A monster!" shouted Lee.

"I am *not* a monster. I'm an ogre!" the ogre sniffed. He looked the children up and down. "And you three look like *strangers*!"

The ogre showed his enormous teeth in a wide grin.

"The King of the Ogres loves strangers," he said. "He'll want to have you for dinner. Follow me." He gestured towards the entrance of a cave.

"Have us for dinner?" thought Lee in alarm.
"No, thanks!"

"Run!" shouted Biff.

Lee spun around and followed Biff towards
the trees as fast as his legs would take him.

When he finally stopped, Lee's heart was pounding. Biff was by his side, but where was Kipper?

"Oh no! He must have tripped and fallen," said Biff. "We have to go and find him."

They crept back towards the cave, keeping a careful eye out the whole way.

"That ogre was big and scary," said Lee. "I bet the King of the Ogres is even bigger and scarier!"

"Don't worry, Lee," said Biff. "As soon as we've found Kipper, the key will take us home again."

They peeked out just in time to see the ogre
disappear into the cave with Kipper!

"We'll have to go in there to get him," said Biff.

"I don't like this adventure much," said Lee
miserably.

Suddenly two more ogres stomped out of the cave. The children ducked down as these ogres stomped past.

"Where *are* those children?" asked one ogre. "The King of the Ogres wants to cook with them."

"*Cook* with us?" whispered Lee. "I don't like the sound of that."

"Me neither!" said Biff crossly. "We're not vegetables, and neither is Kipper! We have to go and rescue him."

Lee and Biff tiptoed to the entrance of the cave.
    "Oh no!" groaned Biff. "There are lots of
tunnels. How will we ever find Kipper in here?"
    Suddenly they heard a shout.
    "There they are!" cried a gruff voice.
"They're going into the cave!"

"Run!" shouted Biff.

They couldn't run back outside because the two ogres were coming, so Lee ran into one of the gloomy tunnels. He followed its twists and turns deeper and deeper under the mountain.

Finally Lee stopped. "Is that far enough, Biff?" he asked. There was no answer. "Biff?"

Oh no! When they were running, Biff must have gone down a different tunnel. Now Lee was all alone in the dark.

He wasn't alone for long. He could hear gruff voices and heavy footsteps approaching.

"Should I run?" thought Lee. "Where to?"

He looked round in a panic and saw a big rock. He ducked down behind it, just before the two ogres from outside stomped by.

"Where is that third child?" asked one ogre.
"The King's making shepherd's pie tonight!"

"Oh no!" thought Lee. "They're making
shepherd's pie . . . but they're using Kipper and
Biff instead of shepherds!"

When the ogres had gone, Lee jumped up.

"That does it," he said to himself. "I will *not* let my friends be made into a pie!"

He set off in the direction the ogres had gone.

Finally he saw a faint glow around the next corner. He could hear the clang of pots and pans being used.

"This must be the kitchen," Lee thought.

He tiptoed forwards.

Lee jumped out into the light of the kitchen and grabbed the nearest thing to hand. It was a frying pan. He waved this around and shouted, "Kipper! Biff! I'm here to save you!"

"Hi, Lee," said Kipper. "Where have you been?"

He was grating cheese while Biff peeled potatoes.

Lee was confused. "I thought the King of the Ogres was cooking with *you*!" he said.

"I *am* cooking with them," piped up a little ogre with oven gloves and a crown. "It's such fun cooking with new friends!"

"Don't worry, Lee," said Biff. "We got the wrong end of the stick earlier. It was all a misunderstanding!"

Lee lowered the frying pan.

"But . . . I thought the King wanted to have us for dinner?" he said.

"Oh, I *do*!" declared the King. "I love having guests for dinner! Tonight we're having shepherd's pie!"

There was a loud cheer from the other ogres. Shepherd's pie was their favourite.

"So . . . there are no shepherds in the shepherd's pie?' asked Lee.

"Of course not!" said the King. "There's no meat at all. We're strict vegetarians, you know!"

Lee realized that he was hungry too.

"It does smell delicious," he said.

When the food was ready, the three children had to stand on chairs to reach the table.

"So how did you like your first adventure?"
Biff asked Lee.

"I didn't like it at all, to begin with,"
answered Lee. "I was cold and frightened
and all alone . . ."

"But now I love it," Lee continued. "And all that running around has given me a *monster appetite*!"

They all began to tuck in before the key's glow told them it was time to go home.